DATING GAME,

a Mary MacIntosh novel

MAUREEN ANNE MEEHAN

DATING GAME,

Copyright © 2024 by Maureen Anne Meehan

ISBN: 979-8-3304-8122-4 (e)

www. maureenmeehanbooks.com

info@maureenmeehan.com

Table of Contents

AUTHOR'S NOTE

Silent shadows now held by night,
Lost voices in an endless flight.

Your laughter faded, your stories unwound,
Yet here in our hearts, your souls resound.

No justice can mend what has gone astray,
No verdict could light the lost light of day.
But you are remembered, missed, cherished, clear as
dawn,
In every thought, tear, and song.

Not forgotten, truly missed, your names remain,
Through whispers, chants, cries, and prayers,
Through gentle rain, light breezes and the rise of the
morning sun,
In quiet echoes and nature's sighs,
You live beyond the "why."

DEDICATION

Dating Game is dedicated to all victims of Rodney Alcala, Ted Bundy, Zodiac, Red Hands, and all other people who feel the wounds of serial killers. It is truly remarkable that there are so many victims. It is not surprising that most serial killers are men, but it is surprising that they can maim at such a high level for such a long time without detection.

This novel is also dedicated to the force of people who seek justice for these victims. You are true heroes.

Chapter 1

"You are so very beautiful. May I take your photograph?"

This was usually the beginning of the end for any woman who met Rodney Alcala.

Rodney Alcala, often referred to as "The Dating Game Killer," was a notorious serial killer and rapist who was active primarily in the 1970s. His disturbing life and crimes garnered this moniker due to his infamous 1978 appearance on the popular game show The Dating Game, while he was in the midst of a killing spree. Alcala is suspected to have killed up to 130 people, although he was convicted of five murders.

Alcala was born on August 23, 1943, in San Antonio, Texas, but he spent much of his early life in California. His family moved to Mexico when he was young, then to Los Angeles after his father abandoned them. Despite an above-average intelligence and high IQ, Alcala had early signs of antisocial behavior. He joined the U.S. Army as a young man but had a mental breakdown, was diagnosed with antisocial personality disorder, and was subsequently discharged.

Alcala's criminal activities began in the late 1960s. In 1968, he kidnapped and brutally assaulted young girls and adult women, showing his lack of specific victim types, which made his patterns harder to trace.

His victims were often sexually assaulted, strangled, and left in gruesome positions.

He would frequently photograph his victims in disturbing poses before or after killing them, which later served as grim evidence in his murder trials.

Alcala was arrested in 1979 in connection to the murder of 12-year-old Robin Samsoe, a case that ultimately led to his conviction.   However, it took decades of legal battles, appeals, retrials, and additional investigations before he was conclusively linked to several other murders. In total, he was convicted of five murders, but he is believed to be responsible for many more.

During his trials, his behavior was often erratic, similar to that of Ted Bundy. At one point during a murder trial, he represented himself, bizarrely asking himself questions and responding in a different tone, which demonstrated his narcissism and lack of remorse.

Alcala often posed as a photographer to lure his victims, using his camera to make women and young girls feel comfortable before attacking them. He was known for his sadistic tendencies – authorities believe he enjoyed torturing his victims, often strangling them until they lost consciousness, reviving them, and repeating the cycle before finally killing them. His known victims range in age from young girls to adult women showing his lack of a specific victim type,

During a murder investigation, police found hundreds of photographs of unidentified women and children, leading to the possibility that Alcala had many other victims, and these murders remain undiscovered and unsolved.

Some families have come forward over the years, identifying loved ones from these images, but most remain unidentified.

Alcala was sentenced to death in California, and in 2013, he was also convicted of additional murders in New York.

He is known to have killed in California, New York, and Wyoming, but it is suspected, based on the numerous photographs of unidentified women, that he killed women and young girls in other states as well.

He died in prison on July 24, 2021, at the age of 77 due to the fact that California does not enforce the state's death sentences.

Chapter 2

Ted Bundy primarily used charm and deception to lure his victims, feigning an injury like wearing a cast or a sling to gain sympathy from women who would assist him with tasks, leading them to secluded areas. His attacks tended to be brutal but quick, lacking the extended torture that marked Rodney Alcala's crimes.

Ted Bundy's crimes spanned across six states: Washington, Oregon, Utah, Colorado, Idaho, and Florida. He frequently traveled to evade capture and strike in new locations. This mobility made it difficult for law enforcement to connect the murders initially.

Alcala's primary crime scenes were in California and New York, though he may have killed in other states. He didn't move around as frequently as Bundy did, focusing mainly on these two areas and occasionally traveling to other states where he stored evidence such as his storage locker in Seattle.

Bundy has been described as a classic narcissist and psychopath with an unusual level of self-awareness, a master manipulator who saw himself as superior and deserving of admiration. His murders were driven, in part, by a pathological need for power and control, rooted in a deep-seated rage, particularly toward women who resembled his former girlfriend.

Alcala, while also narcissistic and sadistic, was diagnosed with borderline personality disorder and had a more erratic, impulsive nature. His obsession with photography and his cruel "reviving" method showed a fascination with life and death, reflecting a need for theatrical sadism.

Bundy gamed infamy as a "celebrity" serial killer due to his involvement in televised court cases and his self-representation, which added to his notoriety. His trials, particularly his final one in Florida were highly publicized, and he manipulated the media's fascination with him.

Alcala's public persona was quieter in comparison but took on a surreal edge with his 1978 appearance on The Dating Game, where he showcased a disturbing charisma while actively committing murders. His court behavior was equally bizarre, including a stint of self-representation in which he cross-examined himself.

Bundy was sentenced to death and executed in the electric chair in Florida in 1989, with his final years marked by public attempts to appeal his conviction and gain notoriety by confessing to additional crimes.

Alcala received the death penalty in California, but due to the state's moratorium on executions, he remained imprisoned until his death in 2021. His court proceedings were punctuated by decades of appeals, retrials, and additional charges as his crimes were gradually connected.

Bundy's case became a textbook study in criminal psychology, especially in understanding the traits of organized serial killers.

His case is often cited in forensic psychology as a case study in psychopathy and manipulation.

Alcala's case remains notable for his extensive photography collection of potential victims and his twisted use of "revival" as a form of torture. He is remembered as a sadistic killer who left an unknown legacy of victims, as law enforcement continues to identify women in his recovered photographs.

Both Alcala and Bundy both exhibited deeply fractured psyches.

Chapter 3

As of 2024, America's most wanted killer varies depending on updates from the FBI's "Ten Most Wanted Fugitives" list. The list includes individuals wanted for crimes like murder, organized crime activities, or terrorism. One of the most infamous killers in recent history was Rafael Caro Quintero, a Mexican drug lord wanted for the murder of a DEA agent, though he was captured in 2022.

Many other fugitives involved in multiple homicides remain at large, The Zodiac Killer has been on the top of the list for decades, as is the Red Hands Killer.

The Zodiac Killer is one of the most infamous and mysterious serial killers in American history. Active in northern California during the late 1960s and early 1970s, the killer taunted police and the public with a series of cryptic letters, ciphers, and phone calls.

Despite intense investigations, the Zodiac Killer was never caught, and the case remains unsolved to this day. He is confirmed to have murdered at least five people between 1968 and 1969, although he claimed responsibility for as many as 37 victims in his letters. The confirmed attacks targeted young couples, and in one case, a taxi cab driver.

The Red Hands Killer concerns the crisis of the Missing and Murdered Women and Girls "MMIWG" across North America.

The red handprint, often painted across the moth, has become a powerful symbol in awareness campaigns and protests, representing the silence around these women's experiences and the justice that is still sought.

This symbol is not attributed to a single killer but rather signifies the ongoing issue of violence against Native American women and the systemic challenges that allow these cases to go unsolved or under-investigated.

There is a theory amongst FBI profilers that there is a "Red Hands Order" which is a corrupt sect within the Freemasons who preserve their power and influence through fear. These cruel men portray themselves as enforcers of brutal, ancient justice, justifying their actions as being aligned with "higher" principles of control and sacrifice. This Red Hands Order sees Indigenous women as symbols of ancient spiritual power and femininity, making them targets to satisfy the order's twisted rituals. This faction, thus, may have adopted the red hand symbol as both a calling card and a tool of fear.

The Red Hands Order wields influence in law enforcement, and they have infiltrated high-ranking positions in local and federal government, effectively silencing cases involving Native American women to avoid exposing this group. They believe that the spirits or power of their victims can be transferred or harnessed through ritual killings. By bringing their victims to Devils Tower or the Medicine Wheel in Wyoming, they carry out ritualized acts they believe will enhance their power, manipulating ancient Native American symbolism for their own gain.

They leave the red handprint as a calling card, both as a taunt and as a symbol to assert dominance, reinterpreting Native symbols in a dark and perverse way that desecrates their original meaning.

Chapter 4

Mary MacIntosh is the prosecutor in the quintessential western town of Sheridan, Wyoming, and she is a tall burnet with wavy hair, beautifully deep-set dark eyes, a wickedly witted woman who is married to the town's sheriff, Burg, and they just had twin boy. She has an immaculate win record as a prosecutor but has unsolved murders of Native American women in her jurisdiction, and this has her deeply upset.

She has been working with the number one FBI criminal profiler, John E. Douglas, to try to investigate and solve the most recent Red Hands murder at Devils Tower in Wyoming, as well as other Red Hands murders within her jurisdiction.

John Douglas was the lead and FBI psychological profiler for the Zodiac Killer, as well as the Rodney Alcala "Dating Game Killer" and Ted Bundy. He was well-versed in serial killers and secret societies, cryptic letters and ciphers.

Mac and John Douglas were trying to trace connections to these murders and the secret society of Freemasons, and the further they dug, the more they uncovered about this secret society that has been protecting certain knowledge, particularly relating to buried casques, or hidden treasures, in North America. John Douglas has come to realize that the symbolism in the casques and the Freemason's history overlaps with certain "ritualistic" aspects found at some crime scenes linked to Rodney Alcala, Ted Bundy, the Zodiac Killer, and the Red Hands Killer.

When he lays this out to Mac and Burg, the three of them arrive at the rude awakening that this monster killer among them is beyond a giant.

These killers share a bond of abandonment, which is a culmination of a dark psychological trauma – abandonment by their mothers, which bred their deep-seated rage toward women. Traumatic childhoods have cultivated these killers' need for control, manipulation, and ultimately, violence.

Chapter 5

Mac could not allow the murder of Sheila SingsWithWolves at Devils Tower to go unsolved and unprosecuted. It was keeping her awake at night. Sheila's body was found covered in blood resulting from over 47 stab wounds. It was an aggressive overkill filled with rage. FBI profiler John Douglas conjured that the murderer was sending a clear message with this murder than he had been abandoned by his mother. He hated Indigenous women, especially beautiful ones like his mother must have been. Sheila was a beautiful Native woman, and he left her with a red handprint over her mouth and the blood was entirely hers. DNA came up empty-handed once again from the FBI forensic team. Whoever killed her did not leave a trace of evidence behind.

Sheila's lifeless body was posed in a dreadful manner, with her legs spread and bent backward in what appeared to be a very uncomfortable position, although the bones were not broken. Not only had she been stabbed, but she had been asphyxiated or strangled as there were deep bruises on her neck. Her eyes were wide open and the red bloody handprint over her mouth was smeared. The positioning of the body reminded John Douglas of Rodney Alcala's victims, and the red handprint conjured the Red Hands Killer. John knew that they had some sort of a copycat serial killer who was blending an amalgamation of former or present serial kills and was accepting the signatures of Ted Bundy, Rodney Alcala, the Zodiac Killer, as well as the Red Hands Killer.

Whoever this murderer was, he was extremely intelligent and extremely dangerous.

Adding to the intrigue for John was that there were dozens of holes dug around the victim, making John, Mac and Burg wonder if this killer was also a treasure hunter, trying to find one of the hidden casques as described in the novel, The Secret. It did not appear that the casque had been found, but someone seemed to be searching for it.

Adding in this new detail made the three of them wonder if there was a tie to the Freemasons and the secret society that Mac recently prosecuted when dealing with the Blood Cresent secretive group involved in the Red Hands murders.

Whatever this was, they knew it was evil and dark and dangerous. There was something eerily different about the murder of Sheila SingsWithWolves.

Chapter 6

As Mac digs into the murder of Sheila SingsWithWolves, she and John Douglas notice the parallels to other unsolved murders tied to infamous killers like Bundy, Alcala, and the Zodiac. They reminisce in the form of flashbacks to these killers' crimes and discuss how these others could be used to show the current murderer's rage toward women, rooted in their respective childhood abandonment issues.

As they were pouring over the evidence in Mac's conference room, the door opened and Mac's paralegal walked in with an open letter in her hand.

"This just arrived via UPS," she said to Mac and John. "I don't know what it means, but it was expressed mailed to you."

Mac took the mail and shared it with John.

"Looks like a cipher," John said to her. "Someone knows that you are involved in this case."

"I don't know what it means," Mac said.

"We will need to scan and email it to FBI headquarters in D.C., as we have cipher decoders there. All they do is decode. They will know what to make of it," John said.

Mac excused herself and handed the letter to her paralegal and asked that she scan and email it to the FBI per John's instructions.

"I think we should send it to the editor at The Sheridan Press to publish in tonight's newspaper. We need the public to see this. It will show that the murderer is targeting you, and it will show that you are working to solve a crime," John stated.

"I agree. I will personally email it to the editor," Mac said.

Mac popped open her laptop and crafted the email with the attachment. It wasn't three minutes before she received a response.

"The editor said that she would rush it for front page news for tonight," Mac told John.

"Good. Your constituents need to know that you are hard at work, and they need to understand the pressure we are under to solve this murder and to try to prevent future ones," John said.

"We need to review our notes and findings regarding the Freemason connection of the Blood Cresent cult and compare these factors to Bundy, Alcala, and Zodiac, and see what links we can tie together," Mac replied.

They put their heads together and started brainstorming.

"I'm going to order us some lunch in, and we can have a working lunch together as we noodle this," Mac suggested.

John nodded.

"I have been eating too many steaks since my arrival here. Can we just order salads?" John asked.

"Sure. I'll call Java Moon and have them deliver two beet salads with goat cheese on spinach," Mac said. "You like beets?"

"I love them," John said.

Mac ordered the food and they rolled up their sleeves with the intent of tying the Cresent Blood cult of the Freemasons with the Red Hands Killer along with the Zodiac copycat who sent the cipher to Mac.

Chapter 7

Devils Tower holds deep significance in Native American lore, often seen as a place of power and mystery. It also was where Sheila SingsWithWolves was murdered.

The Blood Cresent chapter of the sect of the Freemasons was based near Devils Tower, hidden from public view, but functioning as an underground society obsessed with power and control. This chapter practices arcane rituals, claiming ancient roots and connecting them to sites of unique energy such as Devils Tower. This sect believes that they could unlock something through a ritual involving those who harbor deep-seated rage.

John Doughlas heard his cell phone ding, and he noticed that he had an email from the FBI decoder group.

"John, we have decoded the cipher that Mary MacIntosh received and we believe the cipher is an invitation promising understanding and empowerment to a place where the Blood Cresent cult can be free to express their darker selves. The cipher appears to be an invitation to the Zodiac copycat, and to the Red Hands Killer as well as to the Blood Cresent cult for all of them to meet at Devils Tower under the cover of night. They have scheduled some sort of a ceremony conducted by this subchapter of the Freemasons and it is framed as an ancient ritual binding their anger and trauma into a powerful brotherhood that they refer to as their 'pact of blood'," John translated out loud to Mac.

"What the heck?" Mac asked.

John continued reading. "The killers are compelled to 'mark' Devils Tower in some way, tying themselves to its spirit and each other through blood oaths or symbols.

This could signify their commitment to act on their violent impulses together or incoordination, allowing their atrocities to not be isolated incents, but part of a larger, ritualistic purpose," John said.

"So, what you are saying is that this pact could be portrayed as a way for each man to avenge his abandonment through ritual violence, sacrificing women as symbols of the mothers or female figures who betrayed them?" Mac questioned.

John shook his head in agreement.

"So, Devils Tower becomes the epicenter of this pact, a place where they convene to renew their vows or serve as a burial ground or shrine, feeding their delusions of power and unity?" Mac suggested.

"I think you are right," John said.

"I need to call Don Townsend, the head of the Freemasons in town, and ask his opinion on this. He is very well-versed in all things Freemasons. She dialed his number down at the Rainbow Bar on Main Street. As per his usual, he picked up on the second ring.

"Don, this is Mac calling again with more questions for you regarding the Freemasons."

"Fire 'em at me," Don said. For a 78-year-old, he was still filled with spunk.

"Why would Devils Tower hold such spiritual meaning to the Masons?" Mac inquired.

"That's a complicated question with a complicated answer," Don said without hesitation. "It is sacred to Native Americans and it is unique in its formation, much like that of the Freemasons.

It is where Indigenous hold rituals and worship with Mother Earth, but the Freemasons do as well. Add to it the mystery of formation and the mysterious folklore that accompanies the tower. The Freemasons communicate in code, such as the All Seeing Eye on the back of the dollar bill. We have always used code to communicate, as have the Natives. Theirs were in the form of hieroglyphics and ours are similar, yet different."

"I don't know if you saw the Sheridan Press last night, but on the front page is a cipher that I received in the mail. We asked that the FBI decode it, and the decoded message is an invitation for a cult of the Freemasons called the Blood Cresent, as well as the copycat Zodiac Killer and the Red Hands Killer to converge for a meeting of some type at Devils Tower," Mac explained. What would the purpose of such a meeting mean?"

"That I don't know. But it can't be good," Don said.

"No," Mac agreed. "It can't be good, especially in light of the fact that a murder of a Native woman just happened there."

"Yep. I know. Can't be good. I wish I could offer more insight, but I can't. I'll rack my brain about it and if I come up with anything, I will call," Don promised.

Chapter 8

Mac and John were meeting in her conference room after the FBI decoded the cipher. She told John about her conversation with Don Townsend regarding the Freemasons.

"Consider the Zodiac Killer for a moment," John suggested. "Consider his delight, or his copycat killer's delight, in receiving an invitation to a secret society meeting at Devils Tower. "The intrigue of this idea of him being invited to join a like-minded group would appeal to his ego and his deep desire for secrecy."

"Makes sense," Mac agreed.

"Add to in what Ted Bundy would have felt with such an invitation. It would highly appeal to his internal rage and abandonment issues. The concept of him being envied to join this deadly pact that he would likely see as a 'brotherhood' that finally understands him. Continue this notion with Rodney Alcala and what his invitation would do for him. He would view it as a way to become part of something larger than himself. His sadistic nature finds resonance in the twisted Freemason ideals. Now let's cap it off by focusing on the Red Hands Killer, exploring the cultural psychological traumas that fuel his rage. This invitation carries with it a terrifying concept," John said.

"I agree. It's larger than us," Mac said.

Chapter 9

"I just got a call from Burg and he said that there was a guy at Devils Tower late last night digging up stuff," Mac told John as they were combing through evidence in her conference room.

"Casque hunter?" John said without missing a beat.

"That's exactly what I am thinking and same with Burg. The Red Hands Killer was looking for a casque I think after he brutally murdered Sheila SingsWithWolves. We think that whoever this killer is also looking for the buried casque treasure. We are conjuring the concept that maybe this Red Hands Killer used Sheila as an 'offering' to the Devils Tower spirit in order to gain some good fortune to find the buried treasure," Mac suggested.

"I think you and Burg are onto something. I think that there is a connection with the Zodiac, the Red Hands Killer, the Dating Game Killer and the Freemasons, and this cipher invitation is the clue that we have been missing, I will call my team at the FBI headquarters to send agents to guard Devils Tower 24/7," John said.

"Burg is doing the same thing with the Wyoming National Guard,"

"That's a great plan. We know that this meeting is going to likely happen on the next crescent moon, which is in two weeks," John said.

John stepped out of the conference room to make a few calls. Meanwhile, Mac had several arrangements to make in court. She was prepared for them, of course, but her head was stuck in the Red Hands Killer.

Chapter 10

Burg called Mac from his office at the police station on Main Street in Sheridan. "The National Guard used military-like surveillance to unveil the casque. They found it!"

"What? When?" Mac asked.

"Early this morning. They are going to host a news conference shortly at Devils Tower and the National Guard and the FBI have been made aware of the finding. They are going to open the casque on national television, so we will see what everyone has been searching for decades for. I'm hoping that there are some clues in the casque that could help us solve these Native American women's deaths," Burg said.

"We need to attend the press conference," Mac said.

"I'll pick you up in 10 minutes," Burg said.

Mac was waiting in front of the courthouse when Burg pulled up. She jumped into his squad car, and they raced to Devils Tower for the national press conference. John Douglas was sitting in front with Burg, and Mac was in the backseat reading about these secret societies and how they could possibly all be interconnected.

Between the Freemason's sub cult group of the Blood Crescent sect, the Zodiac, Red Hands, Dating Game, and the culmination of "calling cards" left at the murder scene of Sheila SingsWithWolves, she knew that this unveiling of the casque would allow them at least one more clue to help link these crimes of the missing and murdered Indigenous women in America.

Chapter 11

Cameras were rolling when they arrived at the base of Devils Tower. All major networks were present, and they asked for John Douglas, the famous FBI profiler who as a young agent who was assigned to investigate the Zodiac Killer, to take the helm at introducing what this casque unveiling could be, and John readily accepted. He was not media shy and had been the subject of many television interviews and there was even a series called Mindhunter that was based on his investigations into serial killers.

After John made his introduction and spoke about the invitation and the cipher received at Mac's office and what the code meant, he turned his attention to the ceramic casque. He had Burg hold his microphone while John opened the casque. His eyes grew wide with discovery. The cameras panned in closer to see what he was seeing.

"Ladies and gentlemen, it appears that the casque contains a very rare pink diamond along with other items." John tilted the open casque for the media to focus in on another note in the form of a cipher, as well as a small piece of cloth with a reddish-brown handprint stain, and a piece of rock with hieroglyphics etched on it. The hieroglyph was a rendering of a woman at the base of Devils Tower posed in an awkward manner with a knife sticking out of her chest. It was eerily creepy.

Burg then turned to the media and announced, "The cipher that was delivered to my wife's office leads us to believe that it is an invitation for a select cult-like group to gather here at Devils Tower on the eve of the crescent moon in a few weeks.

We will be guarding this area with surveillance, as we need to stop the Red Hands Killer from striking again. The Indigenous women need our protection."

Mac then accepted the microphone from Burg. "We will find this killer or these killers and I will prosecute him or them with every crime that has been committed against this protected class of Native American women. You have my word," Mac professed.

Chapter 12

"Don Townsend left a voicemail while we were doing the press conference and he wants me to call him back. He says that he has some answers regarding the Freemason questions that I inquired about the other day," Mac said to Burg and John as they were driving back from Devils Tower.

"Call him," Burg urged. "We've got to get ahead of this thing before the next crescent moon."

Mac dialed Don's phone at the Rainbow Bar. He answered on the second ring.

"Don here," he said. Short and to the point, per his usual.

"This is Mary MacIntosh returning your call," Mac said.

"You know that question that you asked me about secret societies within the Freemasons? Well, I did some digging and some of the elders from other chapters indicated that they are aware of a sect that call themselves the Blood Crescent Freemasons, and they are a bit off, from what I was told. They believe that if they sacrifice young, Native virgin women, they will be rewarded with strength and power."

"Whoa. That's very dark," Mac said. She had Don on speaker and both Burg and John glanced at each other. "Do you think that it could be true?"

"Yes, I do. The reason that I do is that the Masons have always communicated in code and there have always been different sects of Freemasons. Having a dark, secret society of Masons would not surprise me," Don said.

"Did you happen to see our press conference from Devils Tower today?" Mac asked.

"I did. I had it on the TV at the bar. Customers commented. What a terrifying concept?" Don said.

"It is terrifying," Mac agreed. "If this is what we think it might be, we have a dangerous group lurking, and we have got to shut this down," Mac said.

"You do. You will. Everyone in this town believes in you," he said.

"Thanks, Don. When this is all said and done, Burg and I will drop down to the Rainbow and have a drink with you," Mac suggested.

"That would be grand."

Burg chimed in. "Don, thanks for your help. If you think of anything else, please feel free to call anytime."

"Will do."

Chapter 13

Mac's paralegal entered the conference room where Mac, Burg and John were combing over evidence while sharing a pizza. Burg's mom was there too with the twins, who had learned to crawl and were buzzing around the room and begging for attention, mostly from John. He was a baby magnet of sorts. He loved it. He and his wife of 32 years could not conceive, and they chose to be foster parents to animals instead of adopting a child.

The paralegal handed Mac her research file with raised eyebrows, and then she grabbed a slice of pepperoni and mushroom pizza before leaving.

Mac opened the file and realized why her paralegal looked like she had just had plastic surgery on her eyes.

"Rodney Alcala was a member of the Freemason lodge in California, and reporters from Devils Tower think that his great grandfather was as well, who was also a serial killer, and a Native American, and the reporters are linking the hieroglyph found in the casque at Devils Tower to the Dating Game Killer's lineage," Mac read aloud.

"Holy cow," Burg said. "The pose of the woman on the hieroglyph found in the casque mirrors the photos of Alcala after he strangled and killed women and young girls."

"Didn't see that coming," John exclaimed. "Pardon me, but I need to make a call to HQ."

"What if this secret society of the Freemasons is linked not only to Alcala as the Dating Game Killer, but also to the Red Hands Killer, and the Zodiac Killer, and they are all part of a secret society with ancient rituals that concern power and control over life and death? What if this secret society had the power and influence over other serial killers like Ted Bundy and were the root cause of manipulation, and considered these men as 'prodigies' of them, chosen ones if you will, to carry out heinous acts, rationalizing this as a way to reveal hidden truths or maintain power dynamics rooted in this secret society's history?" Mac asked Burg.

Burg looked at his wife for a minute before reaching down and scooping up one of the twins. He kissed his sweet little angel on the forehead and handed the baby to Mac. He then walked over and scooped up the other baby and held him closely to his chest.

"I think we live in a dangerous world," Burg said. He continued to coddle his baby.

The tension in the room could be cut with a knife.

Chapter 14

There was an agreement among government officials that the pink diamond found in the casque at Devils Tower would eventually be turned over to the Smithsonian in D.C., but for now, it was part of the evidence that had been logged in. It was priceless and did not belong to anyone.

But the precious gem was not the clue. The hieroglyph was the clue and it tied the Freemasons to the Red Hands Killer of Native American women, and it had Mac and Burg and John very worried about the upcoming crescent moon.

An Indigenous woman was killed at Devils Tower on the previous crescent moon, and the Red Hands Killer remained at large.

Chapter 15

In researching the now discovered four casques in the U.S., Mac was ascertaining that each contained clues that linked to the secret Freemason society and she felt an ongoing and growing concern that this dark group spanned centuries and that it was not until the last ten years that these casques had been discovered.

This "plan" of the secret society, whether it was called the Blood Cresent or any other name, was not new. It was orchestrated long ago and simply coming to fruition.

The discovered casques each contained symbols from various cultural and historical locations connected to the Freemason lore. They included hints of murder locations, dating back decades, suggesting that Alcala, Bundy, Zodiac, and the Red Hands Killer were together pawns in a long game by Freemasons all interconnected by these hidden objects. The Freemason "All-Seeing Eye" sign on the dollar bill was starting to make sense to Mac. It was a hidden map, like a suggestion of a scavenger hunt for serial killers.

She pondered the Dating Game Killer. Rodney Alcala enjoyed media attention. If he was a member of this shadowy Freemason society, they could have encouraged him to lean into this fame as part of their dark plot, knowing that it would throw off investigators. Now that she and John Douglas, the FBI Zodiac profiler, were gaining deeper knowledge of Freemason lore, she felt like they might be piercing together clues through hidden casques.

Mac was keenly aware that her own father and grandfather were members of the Masons in Colorado where she grew up, but she didn't know if anyone other than Burg knew about this fact.

As she continued to review evidence, she was coming to terms with the fact that the Red Hands Killer at Devils Tower could be part of a larger scheme, where hidden casques aren't just treasure hunts but markers or offering tied to ancient rituals and revenge. The casques held clues leading back to specific locations and crimes related to murdered Native women, suggesting a darker truth about why these casques were hidden and how they might connect the killings.

Devils Tower is sacred to Native tribes, who have long viewed it as a place of power and mystery. The Red Hands Killer operated most recently at Devils Tower, but she pondered the notion that the killer was drawn there for another reason: to find the buried casque which contained clued ties to these unsolved crimes.

The casque found at Devils Tower linked the Red Hands Killer's victims with the cloth with the bloodied red handprint and the hieroglyph encryption of a murdered Indigenous woman. It dawned on Mac that the symbol of the "red hand" was some sort of an ancient warning about betrayal. It could connect unresolved tribal legends involving vengeance r justice for murdered women. But further, it could like the Red Hands Killer, the Dating Game Killer, the Zodiac Killer, and possibly even Ted Bundy, to the Freemason secret society known as the Blood Crescents, and to Mac, this was horrifying.

Chapter 16

The Freemasons, or "Masons" trace their origins back to the medieval stonemasons' guilds of the 13th and 14th centuries in Europe, where craftsmen worked on monumental structures like cathedrals. These guilds operated as trade unions, with apprentices training under masters who maintained strict codes of ethics and technical skills. By the late 16th and early 17th centuries, these operative guilds began to admit members who weren't stonemasons but shared philosophical and intellectual ideals, becoming "speculative" Freemasons.

Modern Freemasonry, as a fraternal organization, officially began in 1717 with the establishment of the Grand Lodge of England. The movement spread across Europe and the American colonies, becoming influential in political and social movements. Members, including many of the Founding Fathers of the United States, were drawn to Freemasonry's emphasis on Enlightenment ideals, including liberty, equality, fraternity, and reason.

The Freemasons are organized into lodges, where members meet for rituals, moral instruction, and fellowship. Masonic rituals include elaborate ceremonies and symbols, like the compass and square, meant to represent virtues such as integrity and moral uprightness. The organization values secrecy, especially around rituals, which has led to various theories and myths.

Freemasonry has often been controversial, with accusations of secret political power and anti-clericalism.

It has been banned at various times in countries like France, Spain, and Germany, and remains restricted by some religious institutions. However, Masons are clear that they are neither a religion nor a political organization.

Chapter 17

When John arrived at Mac's office, she was awaiting him with coffee and bagels, and she was buried in her research.

"Do you sleep?" John asked her.

"Not enough," Mac replied. "The twins were acting up all night. They are teething, and they are very fussy. I did the three in the morning feeding and I could not get back to sleep. Don't tell on me, but I gave them a tiny drop of Benadryl to get them to settle, and then I went for a run at four in the morning, showered, and here I am."

"Good Lord. I won't tell. My wife gave our girls whiskey on their gums when teething. I thought it was brilliant. We needed our rest."

"That is not beneath me, but don't tell Burg."

"I promise," John retorted.

"I was combing through Freemasonry history, and I'd like to make a suggestion. I think that these buried casques are more than a buried treasure. I think that each one marks a point of vengeance. For centuries, the Freemasons have hidden casques of the site of ancient power, symbolizing a covenant to "balance" the scales of justice. At Devils Tower, for example, I think that the Red Hands Killer has tapped into this dark tradition, believing that killing Sheila SingsWithWolves fulfills an ancient pact," Mac said.

"I know that you have a deep respect for Native Americans," John said, "And I think you are uncovering a disturbing pattern. I agree that the casques could not only lead to treasure but also to sites where Native women have gone missing over decades.

The Red Hands Killer might have twisted this a bit, thinking possibly that each murder is an 'offering' to Devils Tower, believing it will grant him or them invincibility or a perverse form of justice."

"Agreed. I think the Red Hands Killer is using the casques as a guide or ritualistic tool, using this to communicate an intent to draw others to these locations as offerings. I also believe that it is possible that the Red Hands Killer is part of the Freemasons cult-like Blood Crescent rogue faction, acting on twisted interpretations of their code, making this more of a personal mission rooted in revenge or fulfillment of an ancient story about the Red Hand symbol," Mac suggested.

"Then how do we tie the cipher, this invitation to other factions, to this? We haven't talked about the cipher as much as we should be," John said.

"True. I haven't forgotten about it, but I also am looking at the past to try to predict the future, and the future is about the cipher and the invitation, and I do agree that the crescent moon cycle that is upcoming is part of this equation," Mac said.

Chapter 18

"What are you researching?" Mac asked John Douglas as she witnessed him dubiously clicking the mouse next to his laptop in her conference room.

"Red Hands murders over the last 20 years," John answered bluntly. "I need to know everything about these cases, and I have never been asked to look at them before. In fact, I don't think that the FBI has been approached to investigate these cases.

"There have always been jurisdictional issues with investigating and prosecuting the Red Hands murders," Mac said. "The struggle has gone on for decades, and it frustrates not only the Native Americans but also law enforcement and the court system as a whole. Laws are changing, though, for the better, opening jurisdictional confines that have kept law enforcement off tribal lands."

"I find it to be very disconcerting that the FBI has these murders as such a low priority."

"I think the Indigenous people feel the same way," Mac said. "These cases have happened all over the United States for a very long time, and it is truly unbelievable how few have been prosecuted. Now we are staring at one dead-on with Sheila SingsWithWolves, and we have absolutely no leads whatsoever."

"I don't really know where to begin," John admitted. "I have never felt like this before, and I have been an FBI profiler for over 40 years."

"There are no clues at Devils Tower. We only have a deceased Native woman during the crescent moon in a sacred area for Indigenous. That leaves us high and dry," Mac admitted. "And we believe that the cipher is an invitation to four dark subgroups to kill again on tribal land during the next lunar cycle of the crescent moon."

"Savanna LaFontaine-Greywind was murdered in 2017 while eight months pregnant, and her case remains unsolved. Hanna Harris was killed in 2013, and her body was found days later in Montana and remains unsolved. Ashley Loring HeavyRunner disappeared in 2017, also in Montana, and is, again, unsolved. Olivia Lone Bear went missing also in 2017 in North Dakota and her body was found months later in her submerged truck. The circumstances surrounding her death are still unclear. Kaysera Stops Pretty Places was found dead in 2019 in Montana and her murder carries with it suspicious circumstances and remains unresolved," John poured through his notes and read them aloud to Mac.

"Yes, the Missing and Murdered Indigenous Women cases largely remain unsolved and it is an epidemic in the United States, yet it gets very little attention. If any of these murders were the children of a prominent, wealthy, white couple, it would make headline news and all law enforcement would be involved. A perfect example is JonBenet Ramsey.

Her case remains unsolved, but the Boulder Police Department continues to investigate it," Mac said,

"That is a great point. I was assigned that case. I remember if like the back of my hand. On December 26, 1996, the 6-year-old beauty pageant queen was reported missing from her home in Boulder, Colorado, and was later found dead. An autopsy revealed that she was strangled. The Boulder Police Department has followed up on over 21,000 tips, letters, and emails, and interviewed more than 1,000 people in 19 states.

The case has been reviewed by federal, state, and local partners, and DNA experts from around the country. Forensic expert Lawrence Kobiinsky stated that an unidentified male committed the crime. The District Attorney's office also followed the intruder theory. But look at the media attention that case received and the expensive investigation. Heck, even a Paramount+ series titled 'JonBenet Ramsey' is in development I am told and it is starring Melissa McCarthy and Clive Owen as the parents. The series is supposed to follow the Ramsey family before and after the tragedy," John said.

"Wow. I had no idea that on ongoing series is in the works, and this happened in 1996. We have very recent Red Hands murders that get little to no attention whatsoever," Mac said.

"Well, that is all changing with the Sheila SingsWIthWolves case," John said.

"Let's pray that we solve her case, which could possibly lead to the resolution of many Red Hands murders, and maybe we can be the voice of stopping this Red Hands Killer," Mac said.

"I certainly hope so. It is finally getting the media attention that it deserves," John said.

Chapter 19

"In looking at a shared fixation on Devils Tower among these factions, meaning the Dating Game Killer, the Red Hands Killer, and the Blood Crescent Killer, I researched the history of this Native American site, and I think I am uncovering stories of rituals and violence gathering tied to the Blood Crescent cult subgroup of the Freemasons," Mac pronounced to John and Burg.

"We only have six days to formulate a plan before the crescent moon," Burg said. "I feel like we need to hash out a plan that includes the FBI, the Army Guards, and state and local law enforcement so that we are prepared for this allegedly 'invite only' gathering at Devils Tower."

John's cell phone rang and he swiped to answer. The look on his face was grave and serious.

"What's going on?" Mac asked him after he hung up.

"The invitation-only meeting happened last night, apparently. There are four bloody handprints left on the lower east side of Devils Tower near where Sheila SingsWithWolves was murdered," John said.

"Oh dear Lord," Burg said. "If they have already met, then they are serious about formulating a calculated plan of attack sometime soon."

The three of them looked at each other in disbelief.

"We have our work cut out for us," John said, before making some calls.

Chapter 20

FBI onsite at Devils Tower reported that the killers must have met, and through some sort of ritual, they pledged their alliance, each leaving a red handprint in blood as a symbolic oath.

"Do you think that we should go back and check it out?" John asked Mac and Burg.

"You guys can go, but I have too much work to do, and I feel like I've been away from the twins too much," Mac said.

Burg looked at John and said, "Let's do it. We need to get our eyes on this in order to try to put our heads around formulating any defensive plan."

"Agreed," John said.

"Mac, we will stay in touch. Thanks for holding down the fort when I am away," Burg said.

The two men left Mac's office to drive to Devils Tower to investigate.

Chapter 21

Mac's life as a prosecuting attorney with six-month-old twins felt like a high-octane blend of stress, dedication, and juggling intense responsibilities both at work and at home. Each day commenced with a morning routine that started early, with her juggling the needs of two infants, with feeding, diaper changes, dressing, and bathing them after she went on her early morning run. If she didn't put her own self-care first in the day, it would never happen.

Sleep was scarce and interrupted, with the twins waking her up at night for feeding, which left her exhausted and relying on strong coffee and sheer adrenaline to get her through each day. The minute she got in her car to drive the seven minutes to the courthouse, she starting mentally sorting her case files, prepping her court arguments and appearances, and listening to her dictation that she had done the night before.

Her briefcase contained not only legal paperwork but often items for the babies, symbolizing her need to be prepared for both roles no matter where she was.

Her time at the office was filled with non-stop demands, meetings with detectives, reviewing evidence, prepping witnesses, and strategizing for hearings and trials. She was highly focused in court, but stole glances at her phone for updates on her babies from Burg's mother.

When time permitted, she watched a quick video of the twins that grandma had shared, and she tried to call them during her lunch break to check, often feeling a mix of guilt for not being with them and pride for her work.

Mac had pictures of the twin boys on her desk, which provided her with both motivation and a reminder of her challenging wok-life balance.

Her evenings at the office often ran late, sometimes missing bedtime with her babies, which always tugged at her heartstrings. She struggled with guilt, trying to balance her duty to protect her constituents and the need to be present for her family.

She had a reliable support system in Burg, his mother, and her friends. This support system was crucial, yet she felt torn about missing out on early milestones. She was not there when they first started crawling and wasn't the first to see their little white teeth break through the gums.

Once home, Mac grabbed a few hours of work after the babies were put down for the night and asleep. She borrowed her own sleep time to research or review case files that she brought home.

Some nights, she was up bottle-feeding the twins four separate times while feeding, rocking and burping, all the while reading casework while imagining her children's futures. Her life had a surreal pace, filled with both courtroom drama and quiet, intimate moments with Burg and the twins.

This double life of a high-stakes attorney and new mother left her feeling stretched thin, with occasional self-doubt and pure, utter exhaustion. However, she found small, meaningful moments of joy, like when her twins smiled at her, or when she won a case, which helped her reflect on the impact of her work and the impact she had on others' lives.

She hoped that over time, she might start to re-think her priorities, and perhaps come to the conclusion that making time for her children would redefine her personal career goals, even if it meant taking a step back professionally.

For now, she would need to dwell on the struggle and conflict she faced. The biggest struggle was happening at Devils Tower. Solving the murder of Sheila SingsWithWolves weighed heavily on her, as well as preventing any future Red Hands murders.

Chapter 22

Burg was calling her on her cell. She picked up on the first ring.

"The scene at Devils Tower is bizarre," Burg said. "Yes, there are four red handprints that are left on the east side of the Tower, but there are also other things at the base under the handprints. There are eagle feathers, one moccasin with blood on it, beaded necklaces that might have belonged to Red Hands victims, as well as drawings in the dirt in the form of hieroglyphs as if this group wanted to warn us that they are real, and they are dangerous, and that they have a plan."

Mac's stomach turned. "What does John think?" she asked.

"John told me that the eagle feathers at the scene of the Red Hand Killer murder at Devils Tower hold profound layers of symbolism in that the eagle feather is a powerful symbol of the spirit world, hinting that the killer or the crime scene has a spiritual significance. The killer might see themselves as enacting a form of 'justice' or a ritualistic act that ties into the spiritual power of Devils Tower, where the feather acts as a symbolic bridge to ancestral spirits. For Native American cultures, the eagle is a revered creature, symbolizing strength, wisdom, and freedom, as well as a connection to the Creator. The feather might be a twisted calling card, implying that the killer believes they're fulfilling a higher purpose or that they see themselves as a 'judge' acting under a warped belief in ancestral justice."

"I follow that," Mac said.

"There's more," Burg continued. "The presence of the feather could signify the killer's disregard or deliberate mockery of Indigenous traditions and sacred sites. By leaving the feather, they're not only signaling their presence but desecrating a cultural symbol, using it as a dark message to taunt those who would understand its significance. According to John and his other FBI profilers that he consulted with today, this could be especially provocative if the killer has a background that overlaps with or opposes Indigenous culture. For the Red Hands Killer, the feather might represent a twisted personal ritual – each feather left at a crime scene could mark their emotional connection to the crime, reflecting a need for validation or repentance after each murder. They may believe that the feather 'purifies' or absolves them, leaving a pseudo-spiritual token to mask their guilt."

"Were eagle feathers left at other Red Hands Killer murder sites?" Mac asked.

"John inquired today and the answer is yes," Burg said.

"That has never been reported," Mac noted.

"Alternatively, if the killer is Indigenous, it could reveal inner conflict. The feather could be an attempt to ask for forgiveness or even to honor the victim in a tragic, distorted way, showing that they are, on some level, haunted by the killings. According to John, an eagle feather could hint at the killer's intricate understanding of tribal lore, as this site is sacred to many Indigenous tribes.

They might be attempting to draw from the site's spiritual power to 'sanctify' their violent acts or claiming Devils Tower as their own hunting ground," Burg said.

"A calling card?" Mac asked.

"Yes, the feather could be the killer's way of leaving a signature within a deeper coded message, indicating their motives are rooted in a perceived betrayal, loss, or abandonment connected to their identity."

"We keep circling back to the killer's sense of abandonment. Bundy, Alcala, and Zodiac, all share a sense of abandonment from women. Maybe that is what connects this?" Mac asked.

"That's what the FBI thinks. We are getting closer, Mac. But I worry that something terrible is about to happen," Burg said.

Chapter 23

Mac had a terrible dream, and it awoke her in between feedings. She dreamt that there was a showdown at Devils Tower under ominous twilight, with shadows elongating the monolithic structure, casting it as a silent witness to the unfolding drama. The crescent moon was rising, half-obscured by the clouds, casting it as a silent witness to the unfolding drama.

The ancient vow, kept alive by symbols of the casque, the crescent moon, zodiac markings in the dirt, and the eagle feather added weight to her emotions while she slept. She was visualizing through dream a place where nature, history, and death were about to intersect.

She and John and Burg were present in her dream and they had pieced together these clues left by the killers – evidence that leads them not only to Devils Tower but to a place that has held secrets from the dawn of time and that they, too, have taken an ancient vow to protect these mysteries – all at a cost.

As they press deeper, Mac, John, and Burg find a hollowed chamber where another casque lies, surrounded by marks of blood–red handprints. This casque is no ordinary hidden object – it contains documents, and relics, that speak to a hidden truth about the land, the vow, and the killings. She imagines that the killers view themselves as both executioners and protectors, guardians of a truth that they believe would bring ruin if exposed.

They find a written note – a pseudo invitation for Mac and John to "witness" the ancient pact in a sinister manner, inviting them to join or die as part of the vow to protect these secrets.

Suddenly in her dream, voices echo through the crevices, whispers in the darkness from hidden speakers. The killers begin a psychological game, taunting Mac and John with cryptic phrases about "truths hidden in plain sight" and the "price of knowledge." The killers emphasize the symbolism of Devils Tower, hinting that this place has held secrets from the casque. John notes the symbols, drawing on his deep knowledge of criminology and Indigenous lore, realizing these killers see themselves as more than just murderers – they view their acts as guardianship over dark secrets. The Red Hand and Crescent Moon Killers aren't acting alone; they're carrying out a twisted tradition handed down through generations.

The scene feels staged for something ritualistic. The killers have left items tied to their identities: an eagle feather for the Red Hand Killer, and a crescent amulet left by the Crescent Moon Killer and the Zodiac Killer. They find a written note – a map not only to Devils Tower but to a hidden cave. The clues hint at a meeting arranged by the killers, a clandestine "council" held under a crescent moon, where they plan to reaffirm their vow to guard these hidden secrets. Mac, driven by her intense need to protect others, realizes that she is stepping into a trap but she feels like she has no choice.

As they go deeper into the dark cave, the markings on the tocks reveal a history older than they imagined – ancient petroglyphs, eerie symbols of the crescent moon, feathers, and a mysterious circle resembling that of the Medicine Wheel in the Bighorn Mountains above Sheridan. John notes their peril and warns Mac and Burg.

The Red Hands Killer and the Crescent Moon Killer finally reveal themselves, stepping out from the shadows in ceremonial attire, faces half-obscured. They are calm, and certain, believing their purpose transcends morality.

In her dream, a tense standoff begins, with the killers explaining how they are bound by ancient bloodlines to protect these secrets. Casting themselves as the necessary keepers of a dark legacy.

The killers attack, leading to a brutal, close-quarters fight. Burg shields Mac, and John and Burg fend off the killers using their weapons and wit. The setting of the cave at Devils Tower adds to imminent peril in that one wrong step could send them tumbling down the rocks, making every move feel like a deadly dance.

As the fight continues, the killers continue their rhetoric about the vow, the bloodline, and the consequences of exposing their secrets. Their words shake Mac, John and Burg, raising doubts about what revealing the truth might actually mean.

John uses psychological tactics to destabilize the killers, drawing on their emotional triggers – loss, abandonment, and the perversion of the sacred symbols they cling to.

He exposes the killers' inner weaknesses, revealing that their "vow" is rooted in their own twisted sense of power and belonging.

In a final revelation, John tells the killers that the true nature of the ancient vow was never about protecting secrets but controlling others through fear. He watches as the killers' identities unravel when they realize that they have been pawns in a cycle of violence and manipulation.

As the killers falter, Burg seizes the moment to break their grip on power, and overtakes them while shouting that they are not noble protectors but killers using ancient symbolism to justify murder.

The showdown ends with the killers captured and defeated and handcuffed face down in the dirt of the dark cave.

John opens the casque and realizes that it holds dangerous truths about the land's history, ones that people killed to keep hidden. As they walk away from Devils Tower, they're left with haunting questions about whether they've lifted a curse – or merely become part of it, holding knowledge that the killers have been defeated, but these killers may not be working alone.

Mac awoke with a startle, covered in sweat. One of the twins was crying and it was this sound that awakened her. She had never had such a detailed dream before, except when she discovered that she was pregnant with the twins.

It was then that it dawned on her that she was late in her monthly cycle.

Not only was the dream the ultimate nightmare, but so would having another baby at the moment. She darted out of bed to scoop up her crying baby, and as she coddled him back to sleep, she noted that she had another pregnancy test in her medicine cabinet.

She called Burg to tell him about the dream and the details surrounding it. He was shocked by the amount of detail she revealed.

"Burg, are you sitting down?" Mac asked him.

"I'm in bed, Mac, it's early in the morning."

"I think I am pregnant!"

"What? That's not possible! Oh, Lord, I pray that it is true."

Chapter 24

"All rise," the bailiff announced as Judge Maurita Redle entered the courtroom and took a seat on the bench. The bailiff called for the arraignment of the first case of the day. "The People of the State of Wyoming vs. Albert Rogers, Roger ShadowHand, Butch Hart, and Charles Weber."

"Counsel, please identify yourself for the record," Juge Redle said.

"Good morning, Your Honor. Mary MacIntosh on behalf of the People," Mac stated, wearing a black suit and crisp white button-down blouse.

"Good morning. Rosemarie Rodifer on behalf of the four defendants," the public defender announced.

Burg referred to Mac as the "prophet" ever since her vivid dream regarding Devils Tower and how the crime went down. Her dream was dramatically close to the encounter they had with the four killers, also known as the Red Hands Killer, the Dating Game Killer, the Blood Crescent Killer, and the Zodiac Killer. All four were present on the crescent moon at Devils Tower and they were captured inside a cave where they met to plan crimes. Luckily, between the FBI, the Army National Guard, and state and local law enforcement, they went down without much of a fight as they were severely outnumbered.

The charges pending against all four men included first-degree murder, second-degree murder, first-degree kidnapping, and violating the Major Crimes Act, Savanna's

Act, and the Not Invisible Act. Combined, these crimes carried life sentences without the possibility of parole and/or the death penalty in the state of Wyoming.

Mac was unsure that she wanted to go for the death penalty as she knew that it set these creeps up for multiple years of appeals. If she just went for life sentences without the possibility of parole, the appeal process would be swift and these four men would go directly to the Wyoming State Penitentiary in Rawlins, Wyoming.

Obviously, the most serious charge was first-degree murder as the killings were premeditated or occurred during the commission of another felony, like kidnapping. Each defendant was charged with this.

If the killings were intentional but not premeditated, the charge would be second-degree murder, which carries a punishment of 20 years to life. Each defendant was also charged with this.

All of the women murdered were kidnapped during the course of the crime and, therefore, all four defendants were charged with kidnapping as the term is defined as abducting a person with the intent to harm or terrorize, often associated with life imprisonment without parole. All of them were also charged with this crime.

With respect to the Native American victims, the crimes included violation of laws enacted to address the Missing and Murdered Indigenous Women Movement such as the Major Crimes Act, Savanna's Act, and the Not Invisible Act. These laws aim to address violence against Native American women. While these laws themselves don't carry charges, they increase focus on such crimes, potentially leading to more aggressive prosecution and attention.

"How to do your clients' please," Judge Redle asked.

"Not guilty, Your Honor," Rosemarie Rodifer said. "All four enter a 'not guilty' please."

"Very well, then, these defendants are remanded back into custody awaiting their murder trial," the judge stated matter-of-factly.

Burg's deputies had them shackled together in a tether-like manner, and they were led in unison out of the courtroom.

Chapter 25

Burg was worried about Mac in that she was throwing up constantly, and he watched her in court looking pale. She managed to get through the arraignment of the four defendants, but it appeared to be a struggle. After court and during their respective lunch hour, he accompanied her to the doctor's office.

"Ms. MacIntosh, let's take a look at what's going on," her doctor said. They were going to do an ultrasound, despite the early stage of her pregnancy.

Burg held her hand as her doctor, Dr. Becky Harrington, put the gel on her tummy and started moving the wand.

"Everything looks perfect, Mac," Dr. Harrington said. "The good news is that you are exactly on track to deliver in 34 weeks."

"That's great," Mac said, "But it sounds like there might be bad news."

"That depends on your perspective."

"Tell us the bad news," Burg said. "We are prepared to accept whatever that might be."

"It's not necessarily bad news," Dr. Harrington said. "You are having twins again."

Mac burst out crying. Burg had a Cheshire Cat grin on his face bigger than life.

Chapter 26

Mac went directly to her office after the ultrasound and shut her door and cried for 10 minutes. How in the world was she going to manage taking care of the twin boys, give birth to two more babies, and prosecute cases? And then it dawned on her and the answer became crystal clear. She decided at that moment that she would finish out her elected term as Sheridan County Attorney, prosecute this current case against the four killers, and then resign.

She went into the conference room to find John to tell him what was going on. He simply cracked up hearing her lament about being pregnant again with twins. She told him her career decision.

"I think that's great. The town is going to miss such a great prosecutor, but you have to listen to yourself and know who you are. You are spread too thin as it is, and you need to be a mother and wife first," he said.

"I still want a career. I think I might open a law firm and instead of taking cases, I will consult on cases. You have taught me so much as an FBI serial killer profiler, and I think that I could make a decent investigator for hire to consult on cases, and also testify about my findings in court as an expert witness like you do," Mac said.

"Hold on," John said as he dialed his cell. He spoke a few cryptic sentences before handing up. "The FBI will hire you as a consultant post-retirement from office."

"Really? Oh my gosh, that is perfect. Thank you, John. Now I can breathe and focus on prosecuting these animals."

"Yes, you have to put this case together and I am here to help you, and, of course, I will testify in a trial as your expert profiler," John said.

Mac sighed deeply before rolling up her sleeves to get to work on this case. She needed to have her paralegal draft discovery documents such as interrogatories, requests for admissions, etc. while she outlined her trial brief and drafted her trial brief. Rosemarie Rodifer was never prepared for trial, but she already stated that she was not waiving her clients' right to a speedy trial and that the trial would proceed within seven days of arraignment. This did not give Mac much time to prepare, which was Rosemarie's strategy. If Mac could not prove her case in a timely manner, these killers would walk free. Mac could not tolerate this.

She got very busy dictating the discovery requests for her paralegal to draft and discussed strategy with John regarding the presentation of evidence.

Chapter 27

The trial commenced the following week, and Mac was ready to deliver her opening statement first thing Monday morning. She had Burg bring the twins to her office both Saturday and Sunday so that she could spend time with them while working. They were happy babies, crawling all over the place and getting into anything and everything. They loved to pull themselves up on the coffee table in the foyer of her office and grab the magazines and tear them to shreds. They also loved to crawl to her office and dig in the trash, scattering discarded waste all over the place. She had a stack of toys in her office toybox for them, but they rarely showed interest in baby toys. They had those at home. They loved messing with things in her office and they were certainly "monkey see, monkey do" mimics with each other. When one lost interest in tearing up magazines and scooted to her office to create mischief, the other would follow in hot pursuit.

Burg kept a watchful, yet laid-back, eye on them. He let them explore and destroy. He knew that their curiosity and wild abandon were a sign of intelligence, and he had no problem following behind, cleaning their messes along the way. Mac would just shake her head in amusement. They were a two man wrecking crew and this did not bother her the least, so long as Burg cleaned up after them. She didn't have the time to do it.

On Monday morning at 8:30 sharp, the bailiff announced that Judge Redle was about to take the bench. When she walked into her courtroom, one could hear a pin drop. She garnered ultimate respect. She took a seat with a very serious look on her face.

"Where is the public defender?" she asked out loud. Her bailiff shrugged. Mac shrugged.

"Your Honor, I have not heard from her since last week. She did not respond to my discovery requests and promised that she would not waive her clients' right to a speedy trial. I did not receive a trial brief from her, nor did I receive a witness list or jury instructions. I did timely file mine on Friday afternoon, and I had her office personally served with these documents. I left her a voicemail confirming receipt Friday afternoon, but I didn't hear back from her," Mac said.

"Typical," Judge Redle said. "Just typical."

The murderers were seated at the defense table, still shackled.

"Your Honor," Mac continued, I am ready to impanel the jury and get started with my opening statement."

"Can you please call Rosemarie Rodifer," Judge Redle said to her clerk, "and find out when she will grace us with her presence?"

Her clerk nodded and picked up her landline. Rosemarie was on speed dial, as this was a common occurrence, unfortunately.

Her clerk turned and said, "She is on her way up the steps according to her, but that could mean that she's having breakfast downtown knowing her."

Judge Redle shook her head in frustration. She decided to call the arraignment files for the two arraignments she had that morning. Both were quick "not guilty" pleas and the defendants were remanded into custody. Of course, Mac was prepared for both cases in addition to being prepared for this trial.

The courtroom door swung open with a bang, and Rosemarie waltzed in as if she owned the place. She was not apologetic like any other attorney would have been.

She sauntered to the defense table with her briefcase and took her sweet time getting out her files.

"Are you ready to start, Ms. Rodifer?" the judge asked in what sounded like a sarcastic tone.

"Just about," she replied, shuffling files and rifling through a legal pad.

"Do you have anything you would like to late-file with my clerk?" the judge continued.

"No, Your Honor, I don't."

"So you are prepared to proceed on a first-degree murder case for your four clients without a trial brief, jury instructions, or a witness list?" the judge asked in an incredulous tone.

"I am," she said flippantly.

Mac shook her head in confusion.

"Your Honor, I move to have my proposed jury instructions accepted if there is no opposition," Mac said.

"They are accepted and admitted into evidence," Judge Redle said, looking confused and marveling at the same time. "And, for the record, the only witness list is the one filed by the prosecutor, and the only trial brief is also the one filed by the prosecutor. Ms. Rodifer, you have effectively failed to defend your clients, and since the only evidence is that of the prosecution, I believe that Ms. MacIntosh may now move for a directed verdict."

Mac, who had remained standing, said, "Thank you, Your Honor, and the prosecution moves for a directed verdict and we request that all charges be deemed proven beyond a reasonable doubt, and that we proceed to the sentencing faze of trial."

"Granted," the judge said, in a shocked tone.

"Ms. Rodifer, are you prepared to have your clients sentenced sua sponte?"

"I am," Rosemarie said.

"Okay, but I want the record to reflect that instead of simply pleading 'guilty', you have failed to defend your clients, and that is a reportable offense to the Wyoming State Bar. Is it your intention to be disbarred and is it also your intention to file an appeal under the guise of ineffective assistance of counsel?"

Mac's eyes were wide. She had never had this courtroom experience in her career, and she didn't know what to think or do about it.

Rosemarie Rodifer had a sideways smirk on her face. One that confused everyone present in the courtroom, including her clients who now understood why she was setting this up for appeal, but also that they were about to be sentenced to life without parole.

The courtroom chimed in with collective chatter from the gallery, and news reported who were allowed to stand in the back started reporting on the case.

Judge Redle struck her gavel, which she rarely did, and called for order in the court.

This would round out Mac's days as a prosecutor and she would end on a high note. It was the shortest murder trial of her career and the most confusing. She did not see this coming. Not by a million miles.

Judge Redle sentenced the four men as were expected to life in prison without the possibility of parole, and Mac was immediately scheduled to conduct her press conference on the courthouse steps. This case was sensational media attention not only in the U.S. but worldwide. This turned out to be the most epic press conference of Mac's career. She was going out with a bang, for sure.

Chapter 28

Burg was in utter shock when the four defendants were returned to the jail before noon on that Monday. He expected them to be in court all day, and when they were safely back in their cells, he called Mac.

"What in the hell went down in there? I saw your press conference. It's on every network known to man," Burg asked.

"It was the most shocking situation in a courtroom of my career, and likely that of the judge," Mac said. "Rosemarie's strategy might be good for an appeal, but she will ultimately lose her license to practice law, which, as you know, should have happened a long time ago."

"Yes. No idea how that woman passed the Wyoming bar exam," Burg said.

"Me either," Mac agreed. "It's like she did not care at all about her clients or her career. Something is amiss with that woman, but I have always felt this way. She has made my win column sound, but it is unfair for her clients and the criminal justice system as a whole."

"No doubt," Burg said. "Are you going to wrap up and get home at a reasonable time today?"

"Yes, John and I are going to grab an early lunch, and then he is going to help me pack up the evidence, as some of it belongs to the FBI."

"When do you think you can be home?" Burg asked.

"Late this afternoon, no later than four," Mac promised.

"Good. The kiddos will be happy to have their mommy home."

"I will be happy to get down of the floor and play with them. I feel like I haven't played with them much at all lately, and I have not had time to read with them. I dibs bathtime and story time tonight," Mac proclaimed.

"You got it, my love. Enjoy. You deserve it. Make sure you are drinking plenty of water!"

"I promise," Mac said before hanging up.

She and John left her office and walked downtown to get lunch and debrief.

Chapter 29

Mac was excited to hold another press conference on the courthouse steps a few months later. She announced that she would not seek reelection and that she intended to open her own law practice once again and work as a consultant for the FBI. People were shocked by her announcement and disappointed. But her constituents knew that the FBI was gaining one heck of a lawyer and that Sheridan would likely never see a harder-working city attorney than Mac.

She was excited about this new chapter. She believed that she could work from home most of the time and that she could reduce her hours significantly, gaining much more family time.

It was confirmed that she was having twins again, this time two girls. Burg was beside himself. Mac was overwhelmed. She and Burg had gone house hunting with the now nine-month-old twins in tow, as they needed a bigger house. They found their dream house not too far from their current home, and they purchased this home on the golf course as it had a view of the beautiful Bighorn Mountains and it had four bedrooms and four full bathrooms – perfect for a family of six.

Chapter 30

Mac's cell phone rang while she was lying in a hospital bed in labor. The girls were making a special appearance a month early. She had been on bed rest for a month, but it wasn't enough. The girls wanted out, and they were getting their way.

"Hi John, how are you?"

"How are you is the question! Burg just texted me that you are in labor and that the twin girls are coming early. I'm sure that's not music to your ears, but it sounds like it is music to Burg's ears," John adeptly noted.

"He's thrilled. I'm not," Mac agreed.

"I know that my timing is terrible and you can say no, but we have a big serial case at the FBI that I am the lead profiler and I could really use your help," John said.

"What are the facts?"

"This case has been dubbed 'The Midnight Scribe' and it involves a serial killer in Florida. He's been playing a chilling game of cat-and-mouse with law enforcement. The killer emulates the methods and trademarks of infamous murderers, and each crime scene bears a signature touch, like that of Ted Bundy, the Zodiac Killer, Jack the Ripper, etc., and he leaves behind a cryptic, handwritten note taunting the authorities and hinting at future victims," John explained.

"Whoa. Intense," Mac said.

"It gets worse," John continued. "The handwriting and linguistic style eerily matched the Zodiac's infamous letters and ciphers.

I'll send you an email with the FBI case file and summary if you don't mind," John said.

"Send it. I have my laptop with me in the hospital, and my labor pains have plateaued for a minute," Mac said while sucking in a breath in the middle of a sharp pain. "Bug's mom is home with the boys, and he's at work, and I have downtime in my hospital room right now."

"It is on it's way to your email," John said. "Have Burg update me on your progress and Godspeed to your twin girls."

"Thank you, but please take the word 'speed' out of this! I want them in incubate as long as possible, for their sake and mine," Mac joked.

Mac opened her laptop and clicked on John's email that just popped in and began to read.

Chapter 31

John's summary surmised that the Midnight Scribe killer had a fascination with true crime, and his knowledge of famous killers was due to his obsession with serial killers. The handwritten letters which were sent as attachments were a key link between the suspect and the crimes. Each note was filled with taunting clues that seemed to be designed to outline the killer's twisted mindset. They held a strong resemblance to the Zodiac's notes and ciphers. There was media sensation regarding the gruesomeness, and nature of the murders. John relied heavily on his knowledge and skill as a profiler.

Mac continued to endure labor pains while engrossed in reading about The Midnight Scribe.

Chapter 32

"Push," Dr. Weatherington chanted to Mac, "you need to bear down hard. This first one seems stuck."

"I am pushing," Mac yelled back while simultaneously holding her breath, which seemed impossible.

"I'm going to have to use the forceps to get these two out," she explained. "It's going to hurt."

"Aware. It already does," Mac said.

Burg had been called and he was on his way to the hospital, likely with his siren blaring while speeding and disobeying traffic laws.

He bolted into the delivery room while being handed a face mask to affix. He was at Mac's side in no time, allowing her to squeeze his arm and tear his skin with her fingernails.

"Rest for a moment, Mac, and when your next contraction arrives, I need you to push with all of your might, or otherwise we rush you to the O.R. for a c-section, which none of us want," the doctor said.

The contraction was there within 30 seconds, and Mac pushed hard. She heard a loud cry and relief washed over Burg's face.

"Her sister is about to arrive, so please rest again, and when the next contraction hits, push hard."

Again, Mac did as she was told and the twin sister came sliding out, screaming even louder than the first.

"These youngsters have healthy sets of lungs despite being premature," the doctor announced.

Burg was crying like a baby himself, as he wiped Mac's forehead and kissed her gracefully.

"Healthy?" Mac asked.

"Very," the doctor replied. As soon as they are cleaned up and assessed through the Apgar, Burg can bring them to you."

While this process occurred, Burg texted John with the good news. He responded right away with an all-caps CONGRATULATIONS!

"John says 'congrats' to you, my love," Burg said.

"Tell him thanks," Mac said, with her beet-red blotchy face.

Burg brought Mac their twin daughters and he placed them gently in the crooks of her arms. He then kissed their foreheads before kissing hers. One of the nurses was snapping photos of this epic moment in this family's life.

"I'm going to have one of the nurses give you a business card to the urologist that I refer cases for a vasectomy," the doctor said. "This lady cannot go through this again."

"Agreed," Burg said. "I will get myself in there as soon as possible."

"Get it on the books," Mac chimed in while gazing at her baby girls. "Oh, they are perfect," she exclaimed.

"Names?" Dr. Weatherington asked.

Burg said, "Brianna and Beatrice."

"I love it," the doctor said. "Four babies in 15 months all with names starting with a B. Classic."

"What will be classic is that vasectomy," Mac said.

Chapter 32

Mac and Burg were settling into their new house with the new babies. The boys were both now walking and terrorizing the household. The girls were getting into their routine. The boys were obsessed with touching their baby sisters, but they learned to be gentle with them. The boys were clearly not gentle with each other. They wrestled all of the time and loved it when Burg would join the fun.

Mac was working from home full time. She gave up her office space downtown. She had established a large office in the basement of their house, and she could store her files in the rafters of the garage. It was a privilege to work from home and be able to spend so much time with her family.

In the lack of down time that she had, she was able to digest the case that John Douglas had sent, and she agreed to consult with him as a profiler and help him and his team attempt to solve the case of The Midnight Scribe.